RED LIGHT MEAN GO

STEVE RAMBLE

FAMILIAR FILTH

Some old guy wearing open-toed rubber sandals prowls the streets on his Honda Cub. I still don't know what he sells, but I enjoy the familiar sound. He clashes together the fearsome blades of a giant pair of scissors - chang-chang-chang - the aggressive tempo drags my heart rate along with it and a fresh, cold wave of anxiety drowns my comfort. The caffeine-comedown begins. Vietnamese coffee makes crack cocaine seem tame.

The waitress comes with my food. I'm dining with the tourists today at a western food joint. I ordered a toastie, 2 eggs, chopped chilli, and peanut butter and jam on toast. The sinister chilli hovers over the toast, and with a grubby penknife she chops it up into big chunks which land and sink into the yellow jam on the stingy layer of peanut butter. It's not quite what I had in mind, but I translate the situation into Vietnamese and it makes perfect sense.

I eat the peanut butter-chilli-jam toast first out of curiosity; I've heard it's better to assume someone could have some wisdom that you

3

don't. I feel something tickly happening to my foot. I look up. No I don't need a shoeshine, thank you.

"Da khong," I tell the old boy who is sitting on the floor and grabbing at my feet, shaming me for the apparent filth on my freshly shoe-shined shoes. He points at the imaginary dirt, screws his face and shakes his head. He looks like an elderly child; there's no other way to explain it. Maybe he never had a childhood and his body is still holding out hope that it'll one day come. He attempts to fix my broken soles against my will. "No" never works. "I won't pay" is much better. It doesn't matter how good your Vietnamese pronunciation is, or your tones or gestures. The wrong words are the wrong words.

Three 'tre chau' (young buffalo) rip past at a thousand feet per second on Honda Blades. Reliable bikes, built well; they hold their value for years. Complacent hookers perch on the back, sitting side-saddle to maintain some modesty in their skimpy garms, peering through lost, defeated eyes made prominent by the face masks hiding their fake western noses from the polluted air. I feel how they resent the bikes, as their own value diminishes with each journey to the hotel. One of these hooker-delivery boys looks identical to a boy I found in the gutter

4

once up by my flat, except this boy's helmet is still sitting on his head, not yet flung a few metres away to reveal a cracked cranium. Even if you drive fluent Vietnamese, there's always the chance one of the young mafia will turn up suddenly to demonstrate how useless these legally-required plastic caps are, and how vulnerable your skull is.

A few months into my latest stint here I had a young Vietnamese beauty remind me how vulnerable my heart is. I fell for her inevitably because she was a sociopath who enjoyed making men fall in love with her and then torturing them. That may sound bitter, but she actually told me this one night as we lay in each other's sweat and ejaculate, glaring into one another's selfish souls. That's a funny game, I thought. I admired her honesty. At least, I thought, her confession meant I was different, that I wasn't going to be just another of her toys. Her confession didn't mean that. That one really hurt. But I translated the situation into Vietnamese and it made perfect sense. A few months later during a caffeine comedown in a sexual health clinic I realised how vulnerable my cock is. Nothing like chlamydia and a broken heart to put you off dating the locals for a while. We're all so brittle and yet in Saigon we live like tempered glass. I love it.

"Ben-see!" She's back! I act disinterested and continue scrawling into a pink notebook.

"I buy 50 dollah! Ben-see! You buy 10 dollah! Ben-see!" Her marketing techniques are ridiculous and her sales claims unbelievable, and I enjoy every second of our interactions. She pulls out Giorgio Armani cologne and sprays it onto my hand. I pretend to be slightly annoyed and to reluctantly have a whiff. I twist the corner of my mouth and my eyebrows sigh as if to say 'yeah, it'll do.' She offers it for 800,000 dong – 35 bucks American. I offer 150,000, because I want it for 200, and there I stay.

"Ben-seeee!" She whines disapprovingly. I had no idea for our first 3 transactions that ben-see is her modest attempt at saying "these are exPENSIve goods I offer you, sir" – it was a girlfriend who pointed that out to me. I wish she'd never told me, but I don't resent her too much anymore. A few ben-sees later and she goes down to 200. I buy. The stuff you purchase in the markets is fake – same bottles, different liquid. And why go to the malls and plazas when I could haggle with this mad, old, black-toothed darling? Department stores and alleyways – same shit, different toilet. Anyway, the stuff this old lady sells me on the street is 100% genuine, stolen product. Ben-see!

My windpipe tries to vault out through my mouth as I splutter my unhealthy lifestyle into my hands. I feel I'd better pacify my lungs with a cigarette, so I spark up, inhale and watch the dull, red blaze as my lungs settle back into their cot of tar and brake-dust. I look down at the emaciated man coughing up his last breath and clutching his throat on my Marlboro packet health warning. He makes me feel better. I'll never be that ugly, I tell myself. Even if I was, people would still fuck me here because I'm white. All you need is a pallid complexion and a thin nose and you hear 'dep trai' (handsome boy) so often you start to believe it. I vacillate between drinking a coffee or a beer. 3pm is that precarious time when both are feasible, only one is necessary, and the choice will determine the fate of the next 36 hours. I get the Bia Saigon Red because the Saigon Green bloats me and gives me gas, and the Bia 333 tastes like cold piss. I sit in my regret for a minute. It feels warm and familiar.

My best friend Wetwipe arrives. How dare he get involved in this personal moment of mine. I persuade Wetwipe to drink with me. We call him Wetwipe because he always carries baby-wipes and this type of conscious forethought about hygiene is unacceptable, so we ridicule him for it. I call him an autistic; he calls me a pathetic loser who's going nowhere in life, and we have a good ol' chuckle. Of course, this casual lampooning is allowed because we both know he could beat me up if he felt like it. The dynamic is fixed. Men are simple. Remember that height-line you had to stand beside before getting on a fair ride? Wetwipe was once a vertically-challenged eleven-year-old who saw that line as a challenge. He decided that he was gonna be a tall, short man, and now he is. Enough punches to the face and your lips and eye sockets get numb. This is something we have in common. He trained, he competed, he fought, and now nobody fucks with him. Still, I ponder on this man. In fact, I enjoy finding it complexing, that after a year of friendship I still don't know Wetwipe's ratio. Is he a tough, serious character or a timid, sensitive soul? And how much of each? The duality of this man is bipolar. His stern composure is earned through years of self-discipline in more ways than one. I have sincere faith in his research on nutrition, wellbeing and martial arts, but most of all, his honesty. A few words from him have me shadow-boxing at night, consuming raw honey, turmeric, garlic cloves and coconut oil, and quitting masturbation. I ask him how he's doing. He tells me about an argument with his girlfriend where she went silent because he was in a bad mood due to a yeast infection, and then he got snappy with her, so she started to cry because she felt lonely, but he wanted her empathy and felt he deserved it more at that time because of the thrush, and then things inevitably escalated because they both felt like victims. I tell him he was in the wrong. He's pissed off. The wrong words are the wrong words.

We sit and drink, sticking to safe topics of discussion like how to shift your bodyweight and block your face while elbowing someone in the nose. After a while of this amateur MMA talk we're feeling enough empathy for one another to branch out into something sentimental. "You still wanna do this volunteering thing with your girl?" Wetwipe asks me. "Yeah, she talks about it a lot."
"When"
"It's not the right time now."
Wetwipe can smell my disinterest of the subject and he drops it so quickly that I feel ashamed. Instead we dive into pseudo-politics and societal angst. I've recently decided to be right wing. I don't have many right wing beliefs and my ideals are for the most part pretty liberal, but it's not the thought that counts. I say, therefore I am. It seemed like everyone around me was

agreeing too much, and I got bored of us patting each other on the back for our apparent humanitarian opinions while we continued to pursue our decadent ways as the heathens we are. I also want to see if my friends disown me for supporting my prime minister and praising the police and military. You could call it boredom, or even self-sabotage, but I call it anthropology. We head to the local dive bar to play pool and offend backpackers with our non-opinions.

OH ROMEO

I wake up sweating unbelievably, only around the crotch. Shouldn't have worn joggers to bed. I feel like shit. That's not sweat. I pissed myself. Wow. My missus already left for work, and I remember waking up for that, and there was no discussion about pissy sheets, so this must have happened since then. I pissed the bed sober, in daylight. She doesn't know. I hold the power. I get up and have the sudden urge to tell her. I think about the text I'll send. "I haven't wet my bed in years, but last night I wet yours." Nah that's not enough. I settle on saying "I have something to tell you, but I'd rather say it publicly." I then post the news on our group chat, where all of our closest Saigon teacher friends dwell during their more boring classes in public schools. I receive positive feedback almost instantly. They are very supportive. My lady private messages me with some HAHAHAs and questions whether I'm serious. I send the group a picture of the fan on the bed, propped up on a pile of books, directed at the wet stain on the mattress. "I scrubbed it first," I reassure her. More congratulations from our friends; more laughter, skepticism and puzzlement from the lady. She's the one.

Falling in love is my favourite game. It has been ever since I was a kid. It's the perfect mix of chaos and comfort. The sharp vicissitudes of mutual affection and resentment. My sister would say these variable schedules of positive reinforcement create the addiction, like in an abusive relationship. It is addictive, and I'm a very addictive personality. I'm sure addictive personalities don't really exist, and that they're just an excuse, but that's fine. Plus, it sounds better than "I'm an unstable individual with no willpower and a tendency to self-pity and self-medicate, which leads me to underachieve and create tragic relationships." 'Addictive personality' pigeon-holes me just enough to excuse myself from responsibility, and that suits me fine. The right words are the right words.

This latest one is the best one. I know I say that every time, but that's because I always upgrade, every time. I stick to it. This is the best one. A Bolivian Goddess with a surname I can't spell. A determined soul so packed full of dreams that she could burst at any moment. I imagine what this dream-explosion would look like and picture putting a nail-bomb into a butterfly sanctuary. I leave the daydream before I die in it because I'm a quitter. She isn't. She has ambitions to create community art projects and fundraise for the poor villages in the countryside most affected by the recent flooding. I told her I love the idea of volunteering to help the needy, as long I get paid at least a little bit and I don't have to do much work. She has so many ideas that she floods herself. She feels lost and so she follows me. Of course, I suppose she also has an intense adoration of irony. She's an artist in the purest sense. She sketches into her leather-bound notebook onto the thick coarse paper, her fingers flicking and fidgeting as her eyes do the same. She scans something ugly and bland, and her fingers create something beautiful. I think that's why she likes me too.

I will marry her. First I just need money and purpose, and a map with instructions to help me find both these things. Then I'll leave her to venture alone on my quest through the wilderness of potential, to face my ambitions, make my fortune, learn fluent Spanish and to dance salsa, then turn up out of the blue 5 years later while she's strolling through the cobbled streets of Sicily, and get down on one knee. It must be golden-hour, that's the hard bit. After this, all I have to do is bring her to the yacht I'll buy her and sail her off into the sunset. Timing is everything. Of course, I have no ambitions, or enough will-power or integrity for the rest of that stuff, so I'll probably just end up wandering aimlessly around South-East Asia in stained T-shirts.

SAIGON THE TEMPTRESS

Right now I'm an English teacher with too much time on my hands. 'Made in Britain, broken in Vietnam' I write on a post-it and stick on the wall of Note Cafe, my local coffee-hole with a 'write your own note' gimmick. But this is a lie. Vietnam didn't break me; it placated me. I don't even know what my real moral beliefs are anymore. I don't know what I really care about. I want that belly-fire back. My life is far too easy and it bores me. People back home have real problems, the worries of everyday heroes. They have payday-loan debts and mortgages; accidental children and passive-aggressive relationships; laborious jobs and social baggage. There's sincere meaning entwined in these things. I miss them. I feel like a counterfeit human. I get paid too much, work too little, everything's cheap, and I get the women I want because their pickings are slim here for a man who speaks English. "A life of leisure is no life you know" sings Justine Frischmann in my head. Whatever, just Google it if you don't know her - your smartphone's right there. Life without challenge is vacuous. I even started training a martial art to introduce some pain and struggle into my existence, but it backfired and now I'm in the best shape of my life and feel great. I watch in envy at the harrowed, complex, stoic suffering of my favourite protagonist as he overcomes hardships and evolves as a character. I love this film. I order pizza to the house because I can't be bothered to go out. If adversity stopped me on the street here I'd just bribe it to go away.

STAYERS

I always feel like I'm waiting for the perfect time. I'm smart enough to believe there's no such thing, I'm just not wise enough to act on that belief. Like most of my beliefs, I keep them out of the vicinity of my waking life in case they interfere with my ardent self-gratification. Humanitarianism and justice are great concepts when you're spitting hubristic claims at the stranger on the barstool across from you. Everyone's an altruist after 8 beers. I tell them all those saintly values I hold. I can successfully convince my new friend and myself simultaneously that I might not be a self-serving prick. I'll even back it up with proof, given the opportunity. I'll put some vomit-covered, semi-dressed, crapulous girl safely into a taxi. I'll do it vocally and dramatically of course, so everyone around me knows, otherwise what's the point?

"Come on sweetheart! Here you go! Whoopsy, mind your head! Okay, now get home safe!"

Now these other pisshead strangers I don't even like are thinking I'm a great guy, and I feel like Christ himself. Everyone wins except for the girl. She was savagely disrupted from sitting in the gutter spewing over herself, after she'd spent so much time, money and effort to get there in the first place.

I hope I don't sound too bitter. I'd hate to become that old guy who burns himself out here. You meet them around the place. Fat, old Englishmen who give great first impressions: offensive jokes, obnoxious comments to strangers passing by, alcohol dependency - my kind of human. But then they open up about their 4 failed marriages and reveal their prejudices and seething resentment for the culture they live amongst. They bitch about how untrustworthy Southeast Asians are, how the men want your money and the women want your money and your passport. These men seek out the worst of the Thai, Indonesian and Philipina females and forget to blame themselves. How many self-inflicted heartbreaks until I turn into one of them? They glare at waitresses with a putrid mix of lust and disdain. I know a street hustler on Bui Vien street, a 35 year old woman with the voicebox, facial features and vertical endowment of a 10 year old girl. She squeaks "you wan' buy?" at you with a cheeky grin. That's her thing, she's a grown-up child. People buy chewing gum and cotton buds from her because she's cute, like a gurgling baby. Well, I met an old dude that paid to fuck her. I picture her getting home after that ordeal, stripping off the schoolgirl facade and feeling very, very old. These sour, retired perverts are one of the two types of foreigners I hate. The others are the Slackpackers: The travelers who are more than pleased to reap the benefits of a poor economy but then complain about petty little nothings. They'll sit there and pay a few quid for a freshly-cooked meal, freshly-squeezed juice, 4 beers and a pack of cigarettes, then complain about the hygiene standards.

"Ugh they just wash the plates on the street with no soap? That's sooo gross." Umm.. it's also why your food cost less than a pound. The poverty surrounding you affords you this lifestyle so that you can go back to your hostel and piss all over your blog about 'overtouristed' and 'ruined' areas people should avoid without thought to the locals whose livelihoods you're vilifying. Telling the world about 'untouched gems', professing originality as if you'd discovered the New World. Slackpackers are the ones who read one blog post about scammers in Vietnam and decide that everyone is trying to rob them. They accuse the friendly staff of a decent restaurant of overcharging and shortchanging and then go through the itemised receipt meticulously, clutching their handbag. They walk through busy markets with paranoid eyes, staring down anyone who brushes up against them. It's pretty simple to look after your phone and wallet. They're pickpockets, not magicians. I don't know what the third type of foreigner I hate is. I haven't met them yet and don't know if they exist, but I like to keep an open mind.

Here's the thing: If you can't deal with it, go home. Embrace the cholera, the parasites, the dysentery, the corruption, the fakery and forgery, the apathy, the mindlessness, the drudgery and skulduggery, the deprivation, the excess, the pollution and the crime. This is what we live for. This is why we came.

FIRST SIN

Sitting on a really uncomfortable plastic stool with a bruised ass, I watch the local street kids as they endeavour to pickpocket foreigners. These little hustlers are so close to being skilled craftsmen, I just don't get why they chose this place. This is the wrong alleyway; the wrong stinking concrete. These aren't tourists, they're expats. They're not walking around with all their cash in their pockets, unaware of thieving little miscreants roaming the alleys. This dusty-looking boy in the grey polo, though, has talent, the way he goes undetected, stays in the shadows and never lets anyone catch his eyes as he window-shops past handbags and jacket pockets. I spoke too soon. Now he's chosen the two worst marks; a German and a Korean, both sober as hell. I know this because of how articulate they sound as they debate Middle Eastern politics. This little artful dodger has no idea about their sobriety as he doesn't speak the language, and he assumes they are drunk because they speak so emphatically into one another's faces, both trying to drown out the others' voice so they can say what they want to say. The kid strikes, walks close to the Korean and tries to swipe the iPhone from the table. The German notices and stamps his hand down on the phone a split-second before the dirty little hand can grasp it. The kid swiftly scampers off into the crowd. The German lifts his hand, and to the Korean's horror, reveals the twinkles of a smashed screen. Oh well. I get up and follow the little dodger's route. I know where he went. He congregates with some older kids in an alley full of massage parlours and bike mechanics. The way he presents himself I can tell he's the alpha. He's the veteran in this game. I shout after him.

"Oi little brother!" I yell in Vietnamese. All the kids turn and stare at me, ready to scatter. I don't know why I care so much, but I want to help him. I call him out on his mistakes. "One man was Korean, one man was German. No good." The boys stare numbly back at me. Little Dodger shouts back.

"Fuck your mother!" Fair enough, I think.

"They work here! They don't carry much money. Go to busy areas with foreign tourists, not small bars!" At least that's what I think I'm saying. I'm not exactly fluent. They turn and walk away at a humiliatingly slow pace. My cheeks turn red in shame as I realise the reason I followed. I just wanted the street kids to like me. What a sad, sad thing. I care more about their opinions of me than I do my own peers'. Why? They looked like they didn't understand me, or even care to. Usually the kids understand me better than the adults. They're more forgiving of my dodgy pronunciation. I feel like a twat. What do I know about pickpocketing? Why did I approach these little leathered, weathered wisemen? Am I that desperate for a purpose? Do I want to join them? Do I dislike people my own age? I forget about it and head somewhere noisier than my own head. I wonder how a lobotomy would feel. I fixate on the idea of severing the tissue in my prefrontal cortex. It distracts me. I feel lovely. I float silently down the busiest street in the city in search of some drama.

It's not long before I find myself in a negative interaction with a cocky American lad with far too much belief in his intellect. I'm no anti-American, let's get that straight first. To me, hardcore anti-Americans seem like sore losers. They don't hate the US because of their honest views on international politics, their ethics, or views on capitalism and gun control. They hate them because the US is winning the self-confidence game. It's a pathetic reason to despise someone. However, this particular American is a dickhead. Everyone else at the table tries to enjoy a semi-interesting discussion about controlling language and freedom of speech laws. They're all smarter than me so I'm having a great time listening, waiting for my time to disagree with the majority opinion for a reason I'll invent later. The Yank keeps interjecting and talking over people in a sanctimonious voice, and I decide he is my new least favourite person. Other people seem to dislike him too. I try to like him purely for this reason, but it's too difficult so I relax back into conformity and sip my beer. Maybe I have an anti-social behavioural disorder. I wonder if there's an online questionnaire that could successfully diagnose me. The noise starts again. My imaginary lobotomy is wearing off.

I spy the same little pickpocket kids from earlier patrolling the area. I catch the eye of the one I lectured before. He aims a shitty facial expression my way. An energy-saving lightbulb surges with an electrical pulse above my head and just before the filament burns out, I make a "look at this guy" head-gesture, hinting to the cocky American. The street boy looks over at the American, then just glares back at me, but I know he's interested. He hasn't walked away yet. I tap the American on the back and he looks over at me; this is my demonstration of my distraction skills. I small-talk the soul out of myself, asking where the guy's from, if he has siblings, what he studied - all the questions which usually leave a taste of vomitus in my mouth. The American eyes me up skeptically like I'm trying to fuck him. Little Dodger sees this. Expressionlessly, he walks toward me, using a crowd of drunks as a tunnel to pass through undetected. I keep distracting the American, holding his shoulder and making big hand gestures while asking him excitedly to elaborate on whatever tripe he was talking about before. The American shrugs my hand off, discounting me as a stupid drunk, but takes the opportunity to prattle on at everyone again. Now everyone else on the table hates me too. Is this what I wanted? It definitely feels faintly warming in my belly. I don't look down, but in my periphery I see some movement around the American's lap. Our victim continues to spew his self-importance at other bored backpackers. I look around and see the street boy emerge from a crowd a few meters away and head down an alleyway. It's done. Did it work? I abruptly get up and leave the table mid-sentence, casually taking someone else's cigarettes and lighter from the table and not paying for my beer. I follow the boy into an alley and see no one. I turn into a smaller one. Nobody. Down the end is another even smaller alley next to a scummy building with smashed windows. I walk toward it, and in the shadow of the vestibule stands our Dodger, ravaging the wallet like he's unwrapping a Christmas present. This must be his equivalent of my comfortable Christmas morning as a young middle-class blonde British boy, tearing the paper away as my mother gleams warmly down at me with selfless joy in a part-memory, part-TV advert. Dodger sees me and tries to hide the wad of travel-cash, but I've already spotted it.

"50% is mine!" I shout with my basic Vietnamese.

"Fuck your mother!" The kid replies in his fluent Vietnamese. I suddenly gain even more respect for him.

"Work with me. We can make more money."

He runs off. I expected that. Actually I'm lying. I'm deluded, so I expected him to make a deal with me. I saunter off towards home, a little pleased with the new 'pickpocketing' experience, which I shall cross off the uninspiring bucket list I will never complete.

On my way home I decide to get a 'banh mi', a Vietnamese baguette filled with egg, processed meat and pate. When I first arrived here I'd eat it for breakfast, lunch and dinner, but really it should only be drunk people's food for when you know the night has ended; it's their version of a sloppy kebab from the local chippy, and the later you buy it, the greasier it is. I go to my favourite banh mi lady. I have a strong affection for her because she smiles and remembers my name and order. She likes me because I speak a bit of the language, and she grins and starts spreading cream cheese triangles onto the fresh mini-baguette.

"No pork right?"

"Correct!" I tell her. "You remember!" Bless her, recalling my fear of getting parasites and amoebic dysentery again. Her willingness to listen to me speak her tonal language with clumsy cadence fills me with warmth. I feel an aggressive finger prodding my hip. I look down, expecting to see a little girl selling flowers covered in wet PVA glue and glitter. Staring up at me is the little craftsman - the Artful Dodger. Looking at him closely, he seems shorter, but somehow older. The skin on his face is thick and worn, and he has a thick purple scar running down from his right eyebrow to his sharp protruding jowl. He holds out a wad of cash, eyes still fixed on mine. "50%," he says. Of course it's not, but I'm still amazed. I grab the bunch of five hundred thousand dong notes, feeling the thickness and estimating the amount incorrectly. I count it in front of him, not because I want to know, but more as some kind of macho symbol, or to copy what they do in Gangster movies. There's about three hundred dollars worth of dong here. Yeah, the currency is called dong. You get used to it.

"What are you doing tomorrow?" I ask him with urgency, failing to hide my excitement.

"Miss Saigon," he replies in terrible English, referring to the name of the infamous bar, but sounding more like 'meek Saigon'.

"What time?" I ask him in terrible Vietnamese. He walks off. "Okay," I mumble to myself. I walk home happy with my banh mi.

HOUSE SWEET HOUSE

The hems, the hems, I love the hems. 'Hem' means alley in Vietnamese, but these are more than alleyways. The city exists in these winding, tangled pathways. These are labyrinths, widening and tightening like an Alice in Wonderland nightmare. Apparent dead-ends will have tiny hidden offshoots which lead you to courtyards and communities you never knew existed. All life happens here, from the mundane to the debauched, and the neighbours know every detail of all that goes on. You enter Saigon on main roads, and you exit her the same way, and ninety-nine out of a hundred of you will never explore her deeper treasures. When you watch the on-bike camera footage of a motorcycle blasting through the country lanes during the Manx Grand Prix, you feel like you are being "flushed down a green toilet" as my dad says. When your motorbike taxi heads down a hem in Ho Chi Minh City, the U-bend is multi-coloured. Socialism failed to paint her arteries when it coloured the rest of her grey. You zoom past flowers, fruit stalls, restaurants, and little shops selling various coloured plastic goods. A tree is ninety-nine percent dead wood, but the traces of living tissue hidden within are what sustain her ancient body.

I have two padlocks to tackle before I set foot in my building. After entering, any guest would think they're embarking on a live action horror game. Damp, stained, chipped walls and stairways are dimly lit by flickering mucus-yellow lights, barely fixed to the dank ceiling. You wouldn't believe anyone else lived here. Most of my neighbours are hookers and young mafia. I pass them on the stairs sometimes, and they're polite enough. After an average of twenty seconds of wiggling the key around in it's hole, my door can be kicked away from it's wonky frame. Getting home doesn't exactly feel like a relief. Most things function, and I keep it technically clean. The only ornament is a plastic plant, loosely sat in its white plant-pot that's far too large for it. My mattress is solid wood with a dense layer of material on top. I'm a tall, stringy man and my poor lanky spine needs the support. The fan next to the bed is satisfactory at 5am, which is when I prefer to retire to my windowless box; the thick concrete walls have been cooling for a few hours, and the heat is manageable. If I was a productive, go-getting member of the human race, I would be baking in a fan-assisted oven at 10pm while the smouldering sun-heated bricks that wrap around my room turn it into a hell-like furnace. I prefer to leave hell outside my home where I can visit when I feel like it.

My favourite piece of furniture is transient, and comes and goes at her own discretion. Tonight, she lays asleep, sprawled across the whole bed. I take off my clothes and climb in with her. She fidgets, whispers nothing to nobody, and eyes still closed, reaches clumsily for my hand, which I allow her to find. She grabs it and wraps it around herself. She smiles at the darkness. I take in her light. The expression on her face drops. She falls back into her dreams. She forgets who I am, and so do I.

MILK

It all clashes here, romances included. Rich, pale-skinned local girls want the blonde-haired foreign boys who want the dark 'n' dirty local girls who want the tattooed mafia boys who want the blonde-haired foreign girls who aren't sure and want to see the menu again. I know some western guys dating or married to local girls who are well-suited. I know two western ladies in relationships with local men who are also happy. But that means nothing. I know a lot of people. The majority of these inter-cultural experiments have cataclysmic effects on one's sanity. Priorities are a major incendiary. For example, a local female at the ripe age of 24 may be rather desperate to settle down, as her biological clock is tick-tick-ticking and the men think she's almost spent. A 30 year old Vietnamese friend told me he'd never consider a 27 year old woman.

"Why?" I asked.

"She's not already married, so there must be something wrong with her."

"But you're not married.."

"I'm not ready yet. I'm too young!" He chuckled.

And that's kind of how it works. So the locals marry 19 year old girls with personalities pastier than their skin, and the western expats pick up the sloppy seconds from the 'spent' heap. And pretty soon after Joe or Dave or Ben have ordered their coffees on the first date, Linh or Mai or Thanh is talking about how she wants a husband and not just a casual fling. Fair enough. They know what we're like, us horny white animals from the Far West. They've seen the movies. And this is a perfectly reasonable thing to mention on the first date out here. The tragic comedy is that any normal western man will run a mile at this point, as is in his culture to do. Whereas the ones likely to stick around after that shocker irrefutably have something wrong with them. And so the circle of unhappy life revolves around its busted, rusted bearings. I gave up on this East-West disharmony after a few failed attempts. This morning I wake up erect, pressed up against the back of my beautiful Latina. I grab her hips. She stirs, breathes in some life, then turns to kiss me sloppily on my nose and upper lip. I'm always tortured with a mix of adoration and confusion when she shows me such affection. I still wonder why she chose me, and when she'll acquire better judgement. We have some lazy, sensual sex then she goes to work. I stare at the ceiling until I realise it doesn't like me back, and I get up to go and haunt District 1 cafes until my evening classes.

PART-TIME BUDDHISTS

The Big Smog, Sin City, Dirty Old Town, smothered with an abundance of choices for restaurants and recreational activities. I could have gone to a different cafe every day for the last year and I still wouldn't have exhausted the options in my own district, so of course Wetwipe and I frequent the same coffee spots for a few months until we find another one that suits our needs: South-American coffee beans for limiting the anxiety, outdoor shaded seating, and street-chaos to watch and comment on. Today, like most days, we sit and reflect on our environment. Mac, a fellow entropy-adventurer with a more flexible mind than I've ever known, appears out of nowhere, as per usual. He looks like Jesus would look like if he was Scottish and in a Metal band - long flowing orange hair, dark shades and a big unkempt beard. This Mac character is an anomaly, and always a welcome addition to the table. He doesn't give two fucks about your opinions of him, your politeness, your mannerisms. You are either pushing the conversation forward into the great abyss of speculation and confusion, or you aren't. He arrives without plans, and he leaves without goodbyes. I like to ask a reasonable question to this orange-haired lateral thinker while walking through the park, like "hey, you like eating the coconut flesh?" Suddenly he sees it - the Matrix, as Wetwipe calls it. Green code, numbers and symbols, plummeting down at jarring velocity across his mind's monitor, as the variations of interpretation flicker and bleep. Seconds pass as he broods. Finally he responds with "Depends what you mean by 'like'." Okay, here we go. I like this part.

"What do you mean 'depends what you mean'?"

"Well I'm not convinced of 'like' anymore. What the fuck do I 'like'? What is 'like'? It seems that something either satiates a need, like an addiction, so maybe I was feeling below par without it and now I feel relieved with its presence, but is that 'to like'? Alleviation? Or sometimes I'm in a fine mood, maybe a great mood, and something makes that state of mind even better because of some apparent preference, but is that preference real, or just an extension of my good mood? For example, think of a band you've always 'liked' and you claim you 'like' but then you play them one day and you're just not in the mood. Maybe we shouldn't use the generalised "I like" but instead use the present continuous "I am liking" like that Indian guy at the bar who's shit-hot at playing pool always says. Or maybe you play the band you 'like' and you feel like you 'like' the song but really that mindstate can't be discerned definitively as positive, although it's not negative. It's just barely continuing. It's getting you through the day. It's passing the time as your meagre thread of mortality frays and disintegrates in front of your eyes. Is that 'liking'?"

All this from 'do you like coconut flesh?' This is the person you want teaching your kids, not Geoff from Swindon with the goofy jokes. His Yin and Yang stuff is my favourite. It might not be original, but my bet is he came to the conclusion on his own. He's not the type to recite. It was a breezy mid-morning when Mac, Wetwipe and I sat pontificating in front of one of our favourite coffee-holes.

Wetwipe was all like "corruption is bad."

And I was all like "yeah." And so we talked about the cruel disparity of fortune and how unfair it all is blah blah blah and then Mac comes out with a beauty:

"Everything is perfect. It is exactly how it should be." And I straight away loved it before I even understood, because it numbed my inculcated shame and privilege. We asked him to continue.

"Look at this place. It's a fucking mess. It's beautiful. It's a perfect representation of the human condition. On this street alone you'll find the most heartless, malevolent people in the world, and also the most selfless saints. And they all bounce around and knock into each other and make stories happen. It's all happening right here. Stupidly rich mafia throw their Coke cans out of the windows of their Porsches and emaciated slum-dwellers pick them up to sell the metal for dinner money. It makes absolute sense. It's a perfect balance. You can't have too many good people or bad people. It's too unstable. Why are we trying to change it? What do we expect?"

We always try to fabricate easy-read morals around chaos, and it always fails. Is that a segway into this next bit? I just read an article about an English teacher working in Southeast Asia, a young man who was seen by so many as generous and kind. It turns out he used his position to Jimmy-Saville the soul out of every school child and orphan he could find. He did it for years, and eventually confessed to hundreds of victims. I've known a lot of cold, blunt, emotionless men who are never polite or amiable, and they've turned out to be the most sincere, caring humans I've had the privilege to know. The guy everyone calls a racist turns out to have a black wife and kids, and the social justice activist turns out to hate the Jews.

Vietnam stole my trust of good intentions, but I don't miss it. Walk up to that mean old bigot at the bar, buy him a drink, and ask him his story. And be wary of the shirt-tucking teacher at the table who cringes at paedophile jokes. He's hiding something.

TEACHING

English teaching jobs in Asia are transitory positions for most. People either realise they are not suited to the role and take the Midnight Express, or they find a crappy little language center with low expectations and then half-ass their way through each lesson for a year until they're completely disillusioned and miserable. I, on the other hand, actually enjoy it. The job is fun, my company is reliable, the students are high-level speakers, I work evenings and weekends, and I'm paid well. The one thing I find demoralising is the lack of opinions and passion most of my students have, especially the teens. When I was 14 years old I was listening to punk and wanted to overthrow the system; I didn't know what the system was, but it sounded bad, and I wanted it gone. I had a strong, focused disliking of authority and craved rebellion in any shape or form, hence why I'm now wandering aimlessly around sin city robbing drunk people with a child. My students have none of that spirit or angst and it depresses me. They'll probably grow up to be successful and well-adjusted. Poor little fuckers.

Today I'm teaching about freedom. This is one of the better units of the textbook. As usual, I do a mindmap on the whiteboard and ask what freedom means to them. They shout out their answers as I scribble.

"No homewuck!"

"Play game when I want!"

"No extra class!"

"Can go out my friend any tiiiie!" I love this lesson. I've done this with a few classes. I correct some grammar and then we get the textbooks out and turn to the freedom section. I look around and wait for one curious kid to start peeling the forbidden pages apart. There he is, I knew I could rely on little Phong's inquisitiveness. The government came down from the capital a few months back and decided the section of the book which describes Freedom of Press, Freedom of Speech and Freedom of Expression is a threat to the wellbeing of the Socialist Republic of Vietnam. It didn't help that there was a section of the page that explicitly talks about the restrictions of these freedoms for Vietnamese nationals. In response, the Hanoi officials stuck together these pages and slapped the company with a huge fine for daring to infect these innocent children's brains with such thought-crime. The glue was good, and the pages couldn't be freed without ripping them. However, since then, it's been the company's responsibility to paste together the pages of any newly purchased textbooks. The glue they use is useless, and the kids find it exhilarating peeling the pages apart. After Phong starts, the rest follow, releasing this caged information into the wild. My teaching assistant looks at me nervously, and I play dumb as usual. Little Phong speaks up first.

"Teacher, what thiiis?"

"Hmm, I don't know. What does it say?" I ask. Then the class discussion begins. Who stuck these pages together? Why? Is it the same in other countries? What does that mean? I know at some point the son or daughter of an Uncle Ho loving government official is going to run home telling daddy what they studied today in English class, and my work permit will be revoked without explanation. But until then, I'll keep doing it. I don't know if a more democratic future is what they really need or want. I'm not here to inculcate their kids with my liberal agenda, and claim that my way is the best. People demand their own rights, and you can't force them onto someone. Chances are my students will end up studying and living abroad, getting westernised and forgetting the homeland, or if they do decide to champion democracy in their online blogs and at protests, they'll be jailed as enemies of the state just like the rest.

But these are my classes, and I'm not going to forbid someone from reading something that the government doesn't want them to know. That's the government's job, not mine. I don't get paid enough to give up on my few cherished principles. Although, like most, I definitely have a price, and it's shamefully low.

CRIME AN IDIOT'S GUIDE

I'm roaming Bui Vien. Bui Vien is Vietnam's answer to Khao San road in Bangkok. If you don't know Khao San road, you've lived a respectable life and I admire you. Many may have visited for the novelty, become weary of it after an hour, then returned to their hostel. The rest of us are now having uncomfortable flashbacks of lustrous lighting blinding our moral compass, with coruscating images of ping pong balls and vomiting gap-yearers. You wouldn't hang around these places regularly unless you were a masochist. Bui Vien street is self-harm. Miss Saigon is situated in the rotten heart of it - a stain on a stain. This bar is brimming nightly with Electronic Dance Music fiends who spill out onto the street from the sheer density of the crowd within. The exhausted and inebriated huff nitrous oxide from birthday balloons on plastic stools outside. This is where me and Dodger come in. Drunkenness is a handicap, but starving your brain of oxygen is crippling. It's hard to take care of your iPhone while you're blue-lipped and convulsing on the floor. This is the good cop-bad cop routine. I wait until you've taken your NOS inhalation a bit too far - luckily this happens to someone every minute or two - and as you collapse, have a fit, convulse, sway or even just look a bit wonky, I come in as a concerned citizen to save the day. While I nurse you back to a state of health, Dodger goes snatching. I'll make a judgement call on your wallet - how much cash do you carry on a night out? If it looks pretty thick, maybe I'll accidentally knock it onto the floor, where some wretched little miscreant may find it if you're not lucky. We only take the really good jobs, like this solo skinhead melting off his seat, because after a couple of tries we have to move on and not return for a week. After a week, the rotation of wreckhead tourists makes it unlikely we'll be recognised. As for the staff and bouncers, well, they know we work the spot, and we pay for the privilege. Once-a-week per bar is the rule, and it's not our rule, it's Miss Ha's.

Miss Ha is a large, scowling woman who sits at a plastic table on the corner of a hem off Bui Vien. Every now and then someone comes along with a wad of cash and puts it on her table. Tonight it's our turn. Ten percent is a bargain for the protection it buys. The business owners don't bother us, the mafia look the other way, and the police don't even come around. We're untouchable. Little Dodger walks up first and puts down Miss Ha's portion of the cash, then he pulls out three smartphones: two Samsungs and the iPhone. She peruses all three, then claims the oldest one by flopping a fat finger onto it. Dodger pockets the other two. If we only robbed two, she'd have let us have them both. She looks after this street, and the street looks after her. A hand appears and more cash is put on the table. It's the motorbike taxi driver who offered me weed earlier today. Those old moto boys, their scam is real robbery, face-to-face shameless thievery, tricking young ladies into giving them huge amounts by putting the fear into them, taking strange diversions, driving them down quiet hems until they sense the implication of impending rape and they pay whatever the driver asks so he drives her back to safety. How can he respect himself? Miss Ha looks at his demeanour as he pays, then counts our money with her clumsy digit, irritably prodding the notes out of the way as if each plastic slip is an old enemy. She uses her podgy, multi-purpose finger to gesture to her runner-boy, who takes the wads and phones inside. A hooker suddenly turns up, screaming and gesturing into the hem she appeared from. She speaks so fast and erratically that I don't understand any more than the word 'cunt'. Miss Ha sends an iron stare at two young men sat on motorbikes, and without words, the hooker hops on the back of one of them and they're all jetting round the corner towards what I assume is an unfortunate and unforgivable client. Dodger told me Miss Ha's sister runs this street. I assume Miss Ha got the shorter straw and knows it, but it's hard to feel bad for her. She is feared by the entire ward of this district. She is the face of something uglier. Who knows who the sister is. I'd rather not know. I sometimes wish Miss Ha had never met me and I was still just another alcoholic English teacher roaming the crowd and getting pickpocketed by children.

CUANDO

The morning spits hangover-sweat in my eyes as I open them. That dark, brooding expression looks across at me from the other pillow.

"Let's leave," she whispers with wonder and potential in her voice.

"To where?" I retaliate in a dry, dream-cutting tone.

"Anywhere! It doesn't matter!" She answers with more desperation, anticipating my next response.

"But what are we–"

"We can do anything! We can go anywhere! Let's pack our bags and get on a bus! We've got money!"

"You're right. Fuck it. Let's go." She climbs on top of me, and we run away together without leaving the room. I start whispering completely non-sexual things in her ear, telling her all the places we'll go, and all the things we'll do, and it drives her to an intense climax. After cumming we both feel a little more patient. She rolls onto my chest and talks to my claustrophobic heart.

"Let's start looking at flights tonight. We can go and start a project like we said. We can travel around, volunteering in different places along the way. " I lie to her and tell her I think it's a perfect idea. She goes to work and I begin the rotten cycle all over again.

NAUSEA

Today I hate everyone. I hate those people who hang out at the same bar every fucking night just like me. I hate my girlfriend for being so fucking optimistic all the time. I hate this town for making me feel so trapped. I hate the heat. I hate the smell. I hate being hungover. I hate being tired. I hate being sick. I hate that I can't blame anyone else for my state of mind. I hate my actions. I hate this fucking culture. I hate these fucking people. I hate my inertia. I hate me. I am the third type of foreigner. I can't deal with it anymore. I'm going home. Fuck this fucking town. I get up and walk out to the balcony.

I love this place. Sitting on my lady's balcony with a cigarette in my mouth makes me wonder why I do anything else at all. I watch the little old dear next door working in her crappy rooftop garden, legs straight, back bent, jerking upwards as she lifts heavy pots, just how you're supposed to do it here. I think of my grandad in his garden at home, planting tomatoes and green beans in his greenhouse, tending pretty flowers in their beds on the perimeter of his modest lawn which grandma could see through the window

51

from her armchair. An overwhelming sadness uppercuts my ribs. It's been a while since I've thought about such innocence and tranquility. The ache begins to sink deeper into my gut and the icy panic sets in again. I run inside to the stereo and blast some 80s Mexican punk to drown the noise. I down a beer and open a new one. I'm already feeling better. Sensations are dulling, I think it's going to be fine. Oh no, what is that? I'm going to vomit. I feel a stab in my stomach. I cough up a pure, undiluted emotion and cry hysterically all over the floor. It feels like I'm purging a nasty stomach infection. I listen to myself scream out my misery as if someone else is doing it. A stranger. They sound fucking stupid. I pity myself and stop crying. It's hard to continue crying when you've lost respect for your own emotions. Was that enough? Will that short release be sufficient to keep the evil from escaping? I down the next beer and decide to masturbate. After 7 minutes of failed arousal I give up and leave the flat.

CREATING
NEW HABITS

This isn't a job, it's a hobby. Each day Dodger and I go and play our game together, and each score we split fifty-fifty-ish. I'm making an average of four-hundred dollars per night. It's beginning to be all I think about. People-watching has taken a brand new angle. I sit here on Pham Ngu Lao street sipping my macchiato and watch the waves of potential victims pour out of buses from Hanoi and Phnom Penh. I smile at these marks and hope to meet them later on tonight. I choose which traveler looks like the worst person, as if it even matters - I'll only rob the ones which seem the most vulnerable anyway. I justify the thievery by convincing myself each mark is a bad person, creating detailed negative stories about their characters. Projection, I believe they call it. Wetwipe and I are talking to a Slackpacker we met in a cafe.

"I dunno man," the Slackpacker says, thoughtful eyes fixed on the coffee receipt sitting in his nervous fingers. "I don't want to be that guy, but every time they approach me I feel like I'm on the edge of cheating on my girl. Maybe I should stop going out every night." His fingers twitch and fold the paper carefully, revealing his anal-attention to detail. Wetwipe empathises with the very real human struggle this young man is battling. As the conversation turns to reality I detach from my seat, and stagger backwards across the sidewalk.

"What do you think man?"

I stumble into the road, eyes closed.

"What would you advise?"

Smack. A double-decker coach travelling at maniacal speed maims me, hurling me into a karmic state, skull mashed and shattered into rat food, mercilessly splattered onto the tarmac amongst the rest of the filth...

"Dude?" asks Wetwipe.

"Sorry man," I instinctively respond, "I spaced out then. What were you saying?" Wetwipe has no idea what I do each night. His moral compass is too strong to make deluded justifications like I can. Poor guy, living in a prison of right and wrong. As he reflects on this young man's struggle to stay faithful in a long-term relationship, I daydream. The table elongates and their voices become distant. I listen from afar as their faint speech details the dilemma of having so many girls throwing themselves at them but having to turn them all down. This conversation was done before when I still felt connected to doing the right thing. Go and talk to the old me, he'd know what to say. I don't hold any opinions whatsoever on the subject anymore. If you want to do it, do it, my gut screams. My mouth just agrees with them apathetically. Wetwipe senses the cavernous void between us and stops talking to me. I feel something abruptly end, but can't decide whether it's our friendship or my own need for human interaction. Either way it sickens me and I begin to mourn the days when I gave a shit. I wonder if this is temporary, but feel like I already know the answer.

I ALWAYS FORGET HOW TO SPELL BUREACRACY

I love unfriendly people. I love the scowling immigration officers at border-control and the government workers in military uniform who drop my completed form in a pile with the rest even though there are seven members of staff doing nothing behind the desk. I love their disliking of me. I respectfully agree with their judgement of me and move aside for them to strut through the middle of an empty corridor, lowering my head in respect, because that's what they deserve. Why do they deserve it? Because their parents paid for it. Their mothers and fathers saved up their precious pennies from years of working hard ignoring piles of forms and scowling at foreigners and now they're able to pay for their children's jobs. Blissful, womb-like financial security cradles them as they half-ass every task and exploit the working people. This is the way things should be. Do not question it. Do not be friendly. Do not fucking smile.

THERAPY

Nothing fixes self-loathing like the ephemeral bliss of a dopamine rush. Walking into this massage parlour it dawns on me that the main thing that used to restrain me from visiting hookers wasn't guilty thoughts of my girlfriend and the possible damage to my conscience, but the inevitable dent in my wallet. Now that I'm making cash, I skip and dance into this back-alley lady-parlour as if I'm a regular. As soon as I arrive, a young girl greets me with just the right amount of false sincerity. She ushers me to a scarlett couch where I perch and wait. The decor of the house is tacky, filled with trashy leopard print cushions and pink and purple throws, all mismatched and dirty looking. Like every other house here, the true value of the place is made evident by the exposed wiring, the cracked paint and the damp patches on the ceiling. After less than a minute, thirteen working girls stroll down the stairs and display themselves before me in an uneven row. If I ran this place, I'd work on the choreography. Some girls smile, some yawn, and some have had so much work done on their faces that it's hard to tell what emotions they're trying to emit. I choose an older woman that can tell I'm nervous because I think she'll pretend to like me and nurture me more. She takes me upstairs into a pretty standard bedroom that smells of damp and mold due to the inefficient air conditioner. She drags me to a little sink that was obviously installed by a blind, drunk handyman, or maybe they minimised expenses by using one of the girls. The sink leans at a twenty degree angle to the right and it looks like they used wall plaster to seal the gaps in the piping. My woman-for-hire washes my cock with a cheap soap that'll probably whiten my skin and leave my scrotum camouflaged against the wrinkled sheets. She brings me to the unmade bed.

That's it. After this the details don't matter because this kind of scenario only serves to quench a thirst, and after these shameful minutes I'll never look back fondly. Unfortunately, this won't be my last time here.

W H O O P S

I haven't been to class in weeks, so I probably don't have a real job anymore. I've forgotten what most of my student's look like. Only the outstanding characters remain, while the rest fade into half-memories as extras or as the objects in prepositional phrases - "remember when Phuc puked all over that other kid?" or "I was so hungover I swung the door open and it smacked into the face of that quiet girl". We remember the really bad and the really good. Everyone else is just filler. I have imaginary conversations with a class full of my students, all answering in unison.
"HE-llo TEA-cher. How are YOU?"
"Bleeding insanity from my toenails."
"How many people are there in your FA-Ma-LYYY???"
"That's personal. Stay out of my private life."
"Whut doo you DOO?"
"I'm a professional pickpocketer and an aspiring brothel keeper."

Sick and deflated, I drag my feet to Dodger's flophouse. This is where we meet now, the scabby building with smashed windows at the end of a hem in a hem in a hem. I think he lives there with all the other kids. I imagine I'm sensitive young Oliver Twist turning up at this wild hovel filled with little rapscallions rehearsing their methods of thievery on old Fagin. Who is Fagin? Am I Fagin? Abrupt curiosity takes over and I move closer to the worn out house and peer into it. I can see signs of life: plastic buckets, bags of empty cans, a toothbrush resting on a dirty shelf. This is real poverty here, no doubt. I walk around the hovel, avoid the dead rat, and peer into another empty window frame emitting some light. It's a small room, maybe a storage space for all this worthless crap they seem to love, or sell, or collect. Wait, there are four pillows on the floor. Is this a bedroom? Dodger comes into the room. I freeze up out of awkwardness and manage to force a guilty smile, but he hasn't noticed me. He stands right there in front of me, but I'm hidden beneath a blanket of night, whereas he's under cold fluorescent bulbs. I move to the side where I'm less visible. Another little kid follows Dodger into the room, and Dodger tells him aggressively to fuck himself. The boy leaves with no questions. Dodger walks up to the light switch and gets a screwdriver out of his pocket. Is he going to disconnect the lights? Is this a joke? Has he seen me? I squeeze myself even more out of sight, one eye fixed on Dodger.

He unscrews the plastic cover from the wall and reaches inside. He pulls his hand back out. Nothing. I thought this was going to be his money stash, but maybe he's actually just an aspiring electrician. Dodger jams his hand into the wall again; I can see by the look of shock on his face that he's not finding what he thought was there. He drops the plastic cover, screwdriver still in his hand, and screams something I don't understand. The little kid walks into the room again, this time with a terrified look on his face. Dodger grabs the kid and puts the screwdriver up to his chin.

"Where's my money?" He spits into the kid's face.

"What? What?"

"My money!"

"I don't know! I don't know!"

The door crashes open and a short, scrawny woman marches in holding a mop or broom handle or something. She grabs Dodger, and the little kid runs away. Without words she begins whipping Dodger on the arms and body with the long, heavy stick. Dodger cries and tries to wriggle away. The woman's grip is fierce and she continues to beat him.

"Mum!" he screams, "Mum, stop!" Dodger drops to the floor and the woman whips at his legs. He tries to cover them with his hands, curling into a ball, and like any good predator, she zones in on any tender part of her prey, whipping and prodding with the end of her stick. The merciless concentration is terrifying, like she's aiming for a high score on Whack-A-Mole. Dodger's screams turn to a desperate gurgling. He preempts each strike with the fearful noise of an animal in distress. She lifts the stick up for another strike, raises it above her head, then slaps it down on Dodger's neck. He goes silent.

"Stop!" I scream in English. The woman's head rotates like a mechanical doll to look at me, the same numb facial expression and no words. Dodger lays still. She walks up to the window, careful and focused. I notice the track-marks on her arms and the blackened teeth in her skeletal mouth. I'm too angry to move away from her or the stick, so I just stare back, adrenaline pumping through me. This vile crackhead is Dodger's mum. I bet I know who took that money. Dodger begins writhing in agony and whimpering; knowing he's alive and not paralysed removes my anger and brings back my fear in the form of a cold face and weightless knees. In slow motion, the woman smiles the least friendly smile I've ever witnessed, let alone received.

"Foreigner," she mutters in a monotonous croak. One of the first Vietnamese words I learned, but one that will never sound the same again. Then she calmly walks away, stepping over Dodger's feet without acknowledging him, and leaving the room.

"Dodger!" I whisper. What do I do? I can't just walk into the house, can I? I'll make things worse for him, or I'll disappear in that house and never be seen again. I don't know how many more crackheads are there, or if she's coming back. She might be coming back. Fuck it, I climb through the window, get to dodger and put my hand on his shoulder. Dodger flinches, then lifts himself up like a drunk person who's just been thrown out of a bar. He looks at me, then limps out of the room. He's gone into the rest of the house. The rest of this house gives me a jolt of fear that tingles through my testicles, like the sensation of driving too fast over a little country bridge, or dropping down suddenly on a roller coaster, or that feeling when you tip back on a chair and just at the moment you're gonna fall you catch yourself. I jump the hell out of the window, but the hell stays inside. I stay beside the house for a moment, until an ominous silence freaks me out and I instinctively and unintentionally walk away. I'm weak. I'm still that scared little boy taking beatings from the older boys in the park because I can't piss high enough over the bush of stinging nettles.

I can't even look out for a kid. What does that make me? This boy is more of a man than I am. I stay at the entrance to the hem, where I can see other people in the distance. Hearing their voices makes me feel secure because it means they could hear mine if I wanted them to. Dodger appears beside me, red faced and miserable.

"Dodger," is all I can think to say, so I repeat it again, "Dodger."

"Let's work," he responds, and staggers off, semi-broken.

I watch Dodger stumble along on fractured pegs and I reconsider my own baggage. He is the untamed man, with no inculcation of cultural ethical standards, no moral standpoint, and no redundant fear of social stigma. He hasn't been squeezed into a little politically-correct box where he does what everyone tells him. He doesn't feel as if the world owes him something like I do, and he certainly doesn't expect things to get better. He does what benefits him, and when it doesn't, he's out. Gone. The second our little agreement isn't beneficial to him, he'll fucking leave. And so would I.

REGRETS:
'I VE HAD A FEW

There are probably well over ten million people in this city right now. As for us foreigners, the worst of us choose District 1 as our playground. You can go to a busy street here, look down from a rooftop bar, and see the western maggots pulsate and slide around together. From the ground you feel suffocated by the filth, then a few minutes pass and you rub up against enough creatures that the infection is transmitted and you start to assimilate, and then you morph and squirm around just like them.

Dodger walks way ahead, scoping out his next victim. He's not interested in my leadership. I'm not Fagin - I was always Oliver. I'm not even Oliver. I'm one of those cowards who convinced Oliver to ask for more gruel because he didn't have the balls. I never even read the book, I just love the 1968 musical. Dodger spots a few red-faced Koreans in suits outside one of the classier bars. The table is open, there's no real crowd to camouflage against, and I have no distraction powers with these employed types. Dodger is fixed on them. I feel the burning sensation in my temples which occurs whenever I feel something is off. This is definitely off. Dodger is in the wrong place. What am I supposed to do here? I browse the menu, order a beer and sit on the table next to the Koreans. Every Korean has their wallet resting on the table alongside their new phone and foreign cigarettes. They're loud and inebriated, but not stupid. I sit, drink, and wait for some inspiration, but no creative solutions arise and I feel impotent. Pretty soon, I'm halfway through my beer and looking for Dodger in the crowd. Did he move on without me? I look under the Koreans' table and in the mouths of the hems, but he's nowhere. Fuck this, I think. I down the rest of the bottle, resenting the extortionate amount I'll pay for this cheap piss. A little street-seller girl skips up to me asking if I want cotton-buds and chewing-gum. I wonder if her mother is a crackhead too.

"Where are your parents?" I ask in my friendly voice.

"Working."

"Where?" She points up the road. I look at the horde of night-dwellers in the streets and wonder who I am searching for. I ask the bargirl for the bill. Another boy comes up and starts shouting at the little girl; she shouts back and starts slapping him. Suddenly they are having a huge argument,

68

apparently about the place she is selling. Maybe a territory issue? A little turf war? Super cute! A few other kids run up to the scene, both boys and girls, some holding flowers and souvenirs to sell, some empty handed. Everyone is getting involved. A couple of other street kids arrive. Nobody is physically fighting, just yelling. The instantaneous chaos is a welcome relief from the calm of the generic, neon-lit bar. I start to laugh. All the Koreans are watching beside me, chuckling too. The scene is about as dramatic as it could get, like a soap-opera for children, and I have front-row seats to this debacle. I hear a man's anger-filled voice to my right. The Korean is getting involved, and I laugh even more. He's holding a kid by the neck of his shabby t-shirt with one hand, and his wallet in the other. I look at the table - it's bare. I seem to notice this at the same time as the other Koreans, because now they are all erupting into rage and panic, looking around for their precious thumb-scrollers. A wave crashes over the drama and washes all the humour away, and as the tide recedes, all that's left is that familiar sinister odor. The Korean man holding the little boy by the scruff of his neck starts slapping the boy's head and demanding answers from him in the wrong language. The other Koreans are all standing now, and turn to the disruly street-performers with accusatory eyes. One little actor runs to the captured boy and tries to rescue him, tugging at his worn-out vest. One man grabs him. Three more from the gang try to be heroes, but the Koreans snatch them up too. The inevitable happens... inevitably. The rest of the crew, maybe fifteen children, all start punching and kicking the well-built men, and I am amazed at how evenly matched the fight is. It makes sense I suppose; the youth have more to fight for. The Koreans want their material back, but the kids want their freedom. The Korean men start to make a scene, shouting for help from the police. Yeah right, as if cops would ever be walking through this right place at this right time, looking to arrest these right people. I look around, noticing all the foreign eyes watching the scene, and feeling like I should pretend to help the men. I spot Dodger in the crowd, spectating from afar. Isn't he going to save me from this? Can't he see I'm out of my depth here? Dodger stares numbly back at me, giving me the same look he always gives when he's already made up his mind about his next move. I know that something has been planned. He's far more calculated than me. He's a strategic commandant, and here come his troops. Like a swarm of locusts, a herd of kids come crashing through the crowd of spectators, pouring through the gaps in between the foreigners' fat asses, weaving around the audience, all wielding sticks, bats, rocks and plastic piping. In an instant, the Koreans are trounced and beaten mercilessly by an army of Bui Vien's miscreants. Dodger watches; his scar glows neon-blue in the tacky lighting of the bar. The Koreans run away. The kids dash back inside the city's walls like rats that have procured their meal. I slide off into the street with my head down like the leftovers.

WHERE TO?

My heart is beating hard against my ribcage - it doesn't want to support my lifestyle anymore and it's trying to escape. I take quick strides and lose myself down the hems. Dodger catches up with me. The insecure part of me is happy that he cares.

"Let's go to miss Ha," I tell him. I just want my safety, and I can only find it there.

"No," Dodger says. Oh no, please. What's happening? Dodger moves ahead and leads the way again. I follow, because I need him more than he needs me. We end up on the street beside the bus station, where the most unfortunate locals self-medicate, sharing hypodermic needles to treat their sadness. This is not a safe place to be divvying up cash, I think. Dodger stops in the dark by three skinny women, all nodding in and out of consciousness. Then I see her - Dodger's mum. Dodger stands over her, and she looks up at her young man with a vacant stare. She half-smiles, then slumps down into the foetal position. Dodger pulls out the biggest score of cash we've ever earned, and waves it in her face. Her smile broadens and invades her face. I bet she used to be pretty before her teeth got all rotten and her facial muscles died. Dodger puts the money away in his pocket, bends down and picks up a large rock. He holds it up in the air above her head, staring down at her. My eyes feel the threat of its weight, and the gravity makes my teeth ache as the boulder shakes above her mouth in Dodger's hardened little hands. Her smile closes up, and she glares upwards with a dopey, confused expression. Dodger's eyes are committed, sure, dedicated. She closes hers. He laughs, drops the rock beside her head, spits on the floor, and walks away. I follow.

We dawdle past drunken tourists and roadside stalls, cross into the backstreets, wander along dead roads and cross the highway. We spot some plastic stools and stop at an old woman's roadstop; I buy him the disgusting bright-red fizzy drink he likes, and I get a beer. We take them onto a footbridge that crosses the river. Staring down into the black, stagnant water which reflects a distorted, warping image of the streetlamps and neon signs, I find a little bit of peace, and so does Dodger. He hands me half of the cash, even though I didn't earn it, and takes a piss through the railings into the river. I join in, and we laugh as we cross streams. I wonder if we are friends. It feels like something friends do together. I smoke a cigarette, and

Dodger turns to me.

"I want to make more money. A lot more money."

"Okay, but we need to pay Miss Ha."

"No." Dodger walks off, and I stay. This would be a lovely place for a normal person to take his girl. I think of her coming here with her smile, her artist's eyes, her dreamer's mind and her proud walk. I get drunk on my own. I live in catharsis. I mindlessly consume enough beer to blur my vision before the old lady packs up her stall, stacks her plastic chairs on the cart and pushes it into the night. I stumble, directionless, down quiet roads at 3am and find that the only store open sells coffins. I peer into the golden-lit store. Beautiful, hand-carved caskets are conveniently displayed for any late night street prowler, ideal for those nights when suddenly a coffin would really come in handy.

RED LIGHT MEANS GO

Riding with a hangover you really get a sense of what it means to drive Vietnamese. None of that pesky serotonin to remind you of the value of your own life and to stop you risking it all by overtaking a motorbike on the wrong side of the road just so you can cruise behind the next dense herd of vehicles at the same fucking speed. Colours are too bright, everything shakes, quick blurred flash-pans to check your perilous surroundings, a menacing anxiety gripping your internal organs, overbearing heat, itchy paste of sweat and dirt on your face, sickly haze of smog rising up. If someone shifts to the left, so do you. If someone cuts you up, you politely slow down and allow them. If someone rapidly turns left, barely skimming your front tyre and making you wobble, you allow it and take another breath of fresh exhaust fumes. If someone leaves their side-stand down, you shout 'older brother oi' at them and point at it. If someone's left indicator is flashing orange, this means they've accidentally knocked that switch, or were just checking to see the bulb is still working. Attempting to predict the rider's next move based on their signals or position on the road is searching for meaning where there is none. Many have gone down this route and ended up like Steven Wright's fabled protagonist "who went completely insane trying to take a close-up photo of the horizon." Then there's the classic Saigon Kiss: a burn on the lower-leg from a sizzling hot exhaust pipe; you can tell whose exhaust it was by which side of the leg the burn is on. An outside leg burn is a story, whereas an inside leg burn is shameful. Whenever I see any cuts or scrapes on someone in Vietnam I assume it was motorbike related. Bike crashes are so common that it almost seems like a conformist thing to do. Whenever I crash here I get more embarrassed than upset. Hearing a car crash is melodrama at its finest. Heavy machinery screeches to it's vile destiny on wide rubber feet, as crumple zones make deafening crunches that echo through the streets. Moped crashes sound much less heroic. It's more like someone's old CD collection fell onto the floor. Plastic bikes, plastic helmets, and new opportunities for plastic surgeons. Now I'm Just sitting here, being traffic. My cynicism kicks in hard at the red lights. It's the fucking jackets, and not just the ubiquitous 'Fugazi' denim shirt (and seriously, how did the logo of a band who religiously avoided selling band merchandise end up here?) but it's when you're waiting in pain, and someone sitting in the same smog, inhaling the same lung cancer as you, has a jacket that reads "ONE LIFE - LIVE IT!", and next to them a jacket reads "BE ORIGINAL" and the jacket next to them says "BE ORIGINAL". These sentiments don't mean anything any more. Everything I held as an emblem of life-lust or rebellion is now an overly-commercialised parody of itself. The insignia of punk is lost. When I was a kid and I saw a girl with blue spiky hair and a lip piercing I would have fallen in love instantly and dreamed of spending the night throwing stones at old warehouse windows with her. Now if I see someone fitting that description I assume she's a vegan-feminist and she's going to give me shit for my white-privilege. Punk doesn't work in a collectivist society like Vietnam, or in collectivist western sub-cultures either. Punk needs that individualistic egocentrism to survive. Survival is key. Even Johnny Rotten sells butter.

SE VA

I've read blissful paragraphs about the beauty of the female creature, but I've always found the words I come up with are more animalistic. I can't compare a woman to a summer's day or a lotus flower. I started writing about "the poetry hidden within the walls of her hems" once and almost vomited on myself. You only get to say those words if you act on them. People who think lovely things about their lovers but treat them like shit aren't permitted to write poetry until they start sharing the washing-up. I've had unique lessons from each female encounter, and yeah, each twist and bend in my relationships represented a riddle in the never ending puzzle of romance blah blah blah. And maybe the lessons were all put here by a strict God to make sure we earn the privilege of being able to spend our days with the most important creatures on the planet. But I've been learning these lessons and wasting them, discarding my notes on the floor of the classroom, sitting in a chair I built far too tall to reach down and retrieve them. I know how to be good to a woman, but I'm neglectful nevertheless.

Physically I'm still riding through a Saigonese inferno, but in my mind I'm sitting on the old bench, my girl in my arms snuggling her head into my thick woolen jumper, gazing at the bucolic dreamery of my mum's little back garden in England. It's a dismal wintery morning and I'm stewing in my own delight, allowing time to fly as the frost melts on the spider web and reflects the beautiful greyness of the clouds above. I love grey. I've always loved grey. Come summer this garden will bloom into a thousand colours, but the wise grey clouds above will keep it humble.

Still riding with a sore bum. I'll be home soon. In the heat of my bedroom I'll find my sanctuary. She'll be drawing or writing in her leather notebook, and I'll get naked and climb on her and connect with the only part of me left that feels any affection or appreciation. She'll save me and we'll escape this town together, run away to the coast, explore islands, mountains and jungles, and make love on sand and grass and in the ocean. Everything unsullied in my life begins with her. She is my salvation. We'll go to where the maps stop and jump. Why have I been so focused on the idea of making money. Why have I been focused on anything else at all? I'm scared of being happy. She terrifies me because I have a phobia of true contentment.

I'm elated at this sudden realisation. Knowing is half the battle, I'm told. I stop at a market and buy her some yellow flowers and a kilo of avocados because I'm romantically stunted. When I arrive she is wearing my big, green 'Punk is alive and working on a much less ambitious project' T-shirt. Even though she hears me enter, she doesn't turn around. I walk up to her back and kiss her neck, sliding my fingers round to see if she's wearing underwear. She grabs my hands and pulls me round into her line of vision. "I'm leaving Saigon," she reports, matter-of-factly.

"What?"

"I've got a flight and it leaves in a few hours." I look around the room and see she's packed all the bits she's been leaving here. I've always been attracted to impulsive women.

"Why?"

"I've got to move on and do something. I'm going nowhere here, and so are you. I can't just stay in nowhere with you while the rest of the world moves on without me." She notices the ugly flowers and plastic bag of avocados, and the look of guilt in her face breaks my heart. She said it all so straight and to the point, without sugarcoating or drawing it out. I don't deserve any of her regret and she doesn't know it. She deserves the same honesty from me.

"I've been visiting brothels," I tell her, without a moment of thought. After this rapid confession my face starts to heat up and my eyes feel bloodshot as though my body regrets saying it before my mind does. She sighs, takes a moment to analyse my face, then looks directly into my cowardly eyes and tells me the most honest words I've ever heard:
"You know, I'll find it pretty easy to never think about you again." I always admired her determination and self-confidence.

She finishes packing, grabs all her stuff, and leaves me with the droning and moaning of life's repetitions, my own lack of motivation and self-satisfaction, my habit of wandering into brothels, and my knowledge that I'll return to an empty bed. I'll be numb when I close my eyes tonight, but there's always something to look forward to, like the buzz of vomiting your anxiety into the sink at 10am, geared up with enough ennui to repeat all of yesterday's mistakes.

THE BIG STING

Dodger has new clothes. It's never dawned on me until now that he's worn the same outfit every time I've seen him; the same torn, dark blue and green joggers and shaggy, faded, grey polo. Now he's wearing jeans and a white T-shirt, and he's even wearing branded trainers.

"Nice trainers, Dodge!" I tell him in English because I'm too high to speak Vietnamese. He doesn't need to understand the words, and he looks proud of himself. This might even be good for business. Tourists will be much less wary of a well-dressed kid than of a barefooted delinquent. And off we go to work. Just another day at the office.

Peak season for tourism, and the Ozzies are the victims of the night. I've always liked Australians, since backpacking and road tripping through Oz, picking fruit with tough men, partying with posh girls in Melbourne mansions and drinking Victoria Bitter with meth-heads and alcoholics in trailer parks. It's hard to find a more down to earth person than him from down-under. But they're on our turf now, and they're fair game. One good thing about them is they usually have mixed-gender groups. Men and women distract each other, which makes my job easier. Girls carry more cash than guys for some reason, and purses are easier to snatch than wallets. Tonight we're working the crowd at the sports bar while the Vietnamese football team makes the country proud by thrashing the UAE on a big projector screen outside. Anonymity is easy and I'm feeling comfortable tonight, probably partly due to the ecstasy pill I took an hour ago. I play the drunk who wants to "cheers" everyone at the table, and Dodger picks his moment with impeccable timing as per usual. We gather a few devices and a purse and move along. The bright lights of the girlie bars don't seem so nauseating tonight. Screams and celebrations sing into the sky as Vietnam scores. I stand in the middle of the road, lost in my MDMA-induced sense of security. It comes as quite a shock when I'm knocked to the floor from what feels like a blow to the head. I decide it's the Ozzies who have found me and I need to find friends - fast. As if on cue, I see a familiar face, a hard-nut Vietnamese man from Miss Ha's entourage wielding a large wooden pole. He's here to protect me, I think, and I don't try to get up. I decide to watch him avenge me from the floor, as the concrete feels quite comfortable tonight. The man looks down at me and it becomes clear that he is not a friend when he swings the stick at my head again. As the beating gets more severe and each blow to the stomach makes me shit my pants a little more, I think of my mother and what she would feel if she was to see her son in this predicament. The pain only really settles in after the guy leaves, as I'm dragging myself along the floor trying to escape my own battered body, still in my inebriated delirium. Someone picks me up and I wince. A friendly Australian voice empathises with the person he thinks I am.

"Fuck mate, What happened to you?" he says.

"I need a hospital please," I whine.

"Sure, mate. Fuck." He calls his friends over and they all help me out of the crowd. They quickly convince a taxi driver to take my bloody mess into his backseat by paying him far more than I'm worth.

The hospital emergency room is all a bit hazy. I remember lying there with blood pooling into my eye from my head injury for a good few hours, alongside rows of other beds filled with other mangled bodies. I remember being taken for a brain scan and then being forgotten on the journey and left in the corridor for a bit; I remember begging for some water which they kept forgetting I asked for. I remember being back amongst the rows of beds and being told about the bleeding in my brain, and wishing my phone had enough battery to search online for what that means and if it's serious. And then there was the man convulsing in a jarring manner I'd never seen before right at the foot of my stunted bed, making noises I'd only ever heard in Attenborough documentaries, the man's thin hair rubbing against my feet as he spasmed. Then I think I was falling in and out of sleep, then waking to the sensation of the man's balding head pressed against my toes. The weird part was then propping myself up to see a blanket over the man's body and face, and a family at his bedside. I kept my toes on the corpse's head, of course. It would've been insensitive to pull them away.

Now I've got my own large room for some reason, while the locals are all packed in like sardines in the waiting area, some looking like they have minutes left in this world. I guess that feminist had a point about my white privilege. This crusty little room with holes in the wall and a filthy defective sink is luxury compared to what's going on out there. I sit on the edge of my bed, my sore, cut up feet pressed on the floor. I put some weight on them to see if walking is possible. A cleaner comes in, smiling and excited about the foreigner in her workplace. I smile and we exchange niceties without words. She dips the nasty mop into a bucket of dark brown water and cleans up the blood from beside my bed, and as she does so, she wipes it right over the open wounds on my feet. She smiles at me with an innocent "woops" expression and continues to clean. I watch the unsanitary liquid settle into my cuts and it seems far too hilarious to refrain from laughing. I laugh, and it hurts, and that makes me laugh more, and the cleaner becomes nervous and looks away from me. Evolutionary scientists say laughter came about for social reasons, just like Darwin said about blushing. He reckoned there's an evolutionary advantage for the tribe to know that you've committed a social faux pas, or that you've lowered yourself in dominance. Blushing is to let others know you fucked up, so you can't hide it. Laughter is also a social thing. We laugh to tell each other we find something amusing. And what do we laugh at? The unexpected. The punchline that comes out of nowhere, the surprising slapstick moment when the glamorous lady face-plants a large clean window at the mall, or sometimes we laugh from amazement at something happening in a way it shouldn't. We naturally enjoy, and want to communicate our enjoyment of, the unexpected. It's in our nature. I unwittingly communicate my pleasure over this unexpected scenario and the cleaner communicates her complete lack of surprise. From this I conclude that we'll never have enough in common to belong to the same tribe, but I'd wave if I saw her in the street.

LAW AND ORDER

The next time I wake up I am being prodded in my bruised ribs with something hard. I grab it and shout, which was not a good idea, as the hard thing was a police baton, and the person I shouted at was a scowling officer with less humour than the cleaner. I wish she was here now to give a character reference, to say I can actually be quite a friendly guy. The officer punches me in the stomach. I try to curl up into the foetal position but he straightens me out by knocking me in the knees with his truncheon. My eyes open properly and I scan the room, paranoid. As my dad always says: 'Just because you're paranoid doesn't mean they're not all out to get you.' These boys in their beautifully ironed, royal green uniforms are probably all out to get me, I think. There are five policemen in my private room, and the scariest one to me is the one standing at the door, blocking anyone from pushing it open.

"Where money?" Inquires the officer with the stick, speaking broken English in a raspy barking voice.

"What money?"

"Where moneeey?" He prods me deep under

my armpit with the baton and my tender ribs scream, or was that me?

"No! Stop!"

"You pay money now! Fifty million!"

"I don't have fifty million!" Bang! Wrong answer. A swift knock in the testicles sends a sickly throbbing into my stomach. "Yes I do! I do!"

"You pay all money! All!" He barks again in his difficult accent.

"Yes! Okay! Okay!" And that was my interrogation. I must have lasted around ten seconds under questioning. I've watched countless films in which the protagonist perseveres through days of torture, still maintaining a cold look of imperishability even with fingernails peeled off and electrodes on the testicles. I lasted ten seconds. Maybe that's what happens the first time, and you have to practice to build up your stamina, just like when I was fourteen on the living room floor with Clarissa.

"Where money?"

"I can show you! I hide it! I don't use a bank!"

"Where?"

"It's in my apartment! I'll show you where! Take me there! You can take me now," I plead with him because all I want is to be in the safety of my own crappy room right now. He slams a notepad and a pen down onto the bed.

"You write!"

"Okay." I grab the pen and write with care: the address, the floor, the room number, the corner of the mattress under which I hide some of my cash and trinkets. I'm about to pass back the notepad when I remember I only put around twenty million in that spot. Oh no. I continue writing: the plastic plant in the big white pot near the wardrobe. I pass back the notepad which is now worth at least seventy million Vietnamese Dong and half a dozen smartphones – In British money that's around three thousand quid and six smartphones. The raspy-voiced representative of law and order strides out of the room with the doorman, while the other three remain. They instantly relax, and begin to scroll through social media on their phones. I hear one of them playing a shooting game, phlegmatically murdering digital humans, fish-eyes fixed on the screen. I've felt anxiety before, but this is something different. It may be partly down to the comedown from the pill I took, but I start to entertain the thought that I am going to be killed. What happens to murdered foreign criminals in Vietnam? What do they tell the embassy? Maybe I'll go to prison for twenty-five years instead. I feel sick. I close my eyes and try to breathe steadily, just like I did during those nights in a cell back in England. I tried not to think of the shame of my parents or what will happen to me. The shooting game soundtracks my incarceration. I try to go to my happy place, but quickly learn that things are pretty fucked up there too.

The door swings open and two different policemen appear. The screen-gazers look up apathetically.

"Already!" The man at the door says in Vietnamese - meaning 'Done! Finished! Complete!' The officers all walk out and shut the door behind them. It's done, finished, complete. I tell myself to wait ten minutes, and after two, I hobble out in my hospital gown, buttocks winking at the world in the polluted breeze, and I'm gone.

MI CASA ES TU CASA

It's liberating to find your entire habitat destroyed, all your belongings either broken or robbed, and then to check your big backpack to find your final stash -the biggest stash- of cash untouched. They slung the rucksack across the room, but failed to look inside half of the pockets. Only a backpacker would know how many pockets this bag really has. Bless these five hundred thousand dong notes being so compact. A hundred and eighty-three million dong and my precious passport will get me out of here easily. I could start a new life with this.

I head to one of the farthest money launderers posing as jewellery stores and exchange most of it into around five and a half thousand pounds for an exact exchange rate. Ol' Blighty here I come. I hope my parents' dog is still alive. Within hours I've bought my flight ticket and I'm hiding out on plastic stools in the outer-districts, killing time. 'Time Murderer' would be a cool tattoo. Actually, no it wouldn't. Should I get a tattoo before I leave? I sip on my iced-tea and try not to think about Dodger, but now I am thinking about Dodger. Where is Dodger?

SEARCHING...

That boy is my only friend, like it or not. I have other humans to call and talk to, but they're only acquaintances, and they don't know me really, not any more. They only know who I pretend to be. They see my occasional wit and enthusiasm, my charm and seduction, but only Dodger knows every trace of the greedy, villainous wretch I've become. He is a witness to my actions, and very few of my words, and therefore judges me accurately. I'm scared they caught him too on Bui Vien that night, and put him in a juvenile detention centre. I imagine a sketchy borstal where the roughneck kids all battle for mere survival. I don't know anything about Vietnam's criminal justice system so my mind creates what it wants. Trepidation binds me to the safe, plastic chair at the thought of going over to that broken little house in a hem in a hem in a hem to behold that rotten old child-beater again. I tell myself I'll never return to that place. Never. I tell myself over and over in my mind because it distracts and soothes me and makes the ride over there seem much faster. I pull up on my bike, ready to make my getaway. I'm not getting off the bike. "Dodger!" I yell, ready for anything. I yell a few times with no response. I get off the bike and peer through the window that still stinks of foul memories. The room is bare, aside from some tin foil and a dirty blanket on the floor. It's empty. I'm not going in there. I push the front door open with ease. Nothing and no one inside scares the hell into me, and the hell doesn't come out. Slowly treading through the nasty house I feel something pull me away. I walk backwards through the front door and the hell finally leaves me. I get on the bike and jet off, hoping the breeze will cleanse my aura.

Prowling the streets of Sin City once again, I feel at home, like I could just fall back into this life once more. I take in the delicious aroma of decaying meat heating under the angry sun. Home is where you can appreciate the ugliness. This is Dodger's home. This is my home. I pass the bus station where the addicts and the radics coalesce. If I see Dodger's mum, maybe I can sober her up and ask where her son is. Sometimes we choose stupid ideas because there are no smart ones left. I park up to stroll the stained sidewalk, traversing needles, foil, dreams and disappointments. The sparse, sedated crowd gets younger and more populated as I walk, as though I'm traveling backwards along a timeline of misery. So many teenage addicts, but not a lot of elderly ones. I guess it's an achievement for junkies to reach old age, although I feel they probably cheated and started the race half way. The next thing I see hurts more than any beating, and breaks my heart more than losing my girl. Dodger lays there, pale faced and squinty-eyed. He looks grey. I've always hated grey. He's resting his head on an old man's sleeping feet. He reminds me of my corpse neighbour in the hospital waiting room. Tin foil surrounds him, and I recognise some of his inebriated friends. They look like they've been sitting in vinegar for a month - pickled children. I pick Dodger up and take him to my bike. I sit him on my lap like a baby, put the helmet on his little dirty head and tighten the strap. We ride.

Silence accompanies us as we glide along tarmac, absent of thoughts. City, suburbs, highway, countryside - freedom. No concrete confines us and no fumes defile our noses. Steadily we ride, until the landscape feels foreign. Green is everywhere. We sit beside a rice paddy on some plastic seats for some noodle soup. Dodger makes no complaints as I force him to eat. He struggles to swallow the Pho, but I can see the life returning to his face. We watch the farmers harvest their seasonal winnings with honest hands and exhausted spines. I'm not a religious person, but if there is a heaven, we're driving in the right direction. The villages and its inhabitants are the reason I fell in love with this country in the first place. This is real life, right here, and the city is a simulation of what life might be like if we were all worse people. Saigon is nothing but a game we play as fictional characters, and you have to leave the game to win.

I have a broken conversation with the aunty who made our dinner, as she asks me where I'm from and what's wrong with Dodger. I tell her he's my wife's little brother and he's sick. She fetches him some fresh sugarcane water and tells him to drink. I ask her about the rice harvest and she giggles and explains to me that there are many different words for rice, depending on whether it's a young plant, ready to be picked, picked and still in the kernel, ready to cook, or cooked. I tell her I think we only have one. She laughs, and so do I. We're both enjoying the surprise. We thank the aunty for the delicious food and continue on our pilgrimage. She waves and thanks me for bestowing my Godly, foreign self upon her business. These aren't her exact words, but her friendliness shows me how rarely, if ever, she meets a foreign person. If only she knew the truth about what I've been doing to her beloved nation, she'd spit at my feet.

By the time we reach the ocean, the sun has painted the sky with a pink and purple farewell. It dawns on my lucky, naive brain that this is probably Dodger's first time at the seaside. He looks in wonder at the waves bashing the fine white sand at our feet. I get up, get down to boxers, then wade in through the shore break to take a dip. My cuts sting and my bruises ache, but tranquility and inner-peace tease me, trying to break the surface, like fish nibbling at dead skin. I float on my back with my ears submerged in the cool water, eyes closed, creating my own sensory deprivation tank. Peace at last. Time passes as the tide rises. A beautiful feeling of elevation makes my stomach jump, which turns out to be a shore-crashing wave blasting me out of the sea aggressively and slamming me onto the sand. I laugh at myself, feeling winded, stinging and aching a little more than before. I've missed laughing at myself. I crawl up to safety and lay on the sand, and Dodger continues staring at the blue crystals in the water, like sapphires winking at him. He scans the golden beach and the small, circular fishing boats being prepared by leather-skinned men fixing their fishing nets for that evening's mission. I wonder what he's thinking. I have an excellent idea, I think. I pick him up and carry him over to the sea.

"Fuck your mother!" he screams as he squirms in my hands. I've missed those words. I take us both past the crashing waves and swim us a few meters out, holding him up as he kicks and yells frantically.

"Relax!" I tell him. He slows down a bit and looks at me expectantly. I realise he trusts me. What a strange feeling in my throat. I submerge his skinny body a little bit, holding his torso firmly up.

"Swim!"

"No!"

"Swim!" I yell at him, and he begins to paddle and kick – clumsily, but determined. The motion pulls him gently away from my hand. I let him go, and he moves a bit on his own before beginning to submerge. I catch him. "Well done!" I shout, ecstatic. The lump in my throat is very real.

"Fuck your mother!" I take him back to the beach as carefully as I can, but the sea spits us out and I land hard on the sand. I look up at him. He stands up and looks down at me. He kicks sand into my face, and I feel it hit my teeth. I spit. He laughs. I throw sand back at him and he runs away, giggling. I chase him, and as I gain on him with a handful of sand, his giggles turn high-pitched and he fights back, throwing the sand blindly backwards at me without aim, like only a child would do. I sit down and my tongue searches for the remaining grains of sand between my teeth. Dodger is still excited and kicks sand around randomly, picking up shells and washed-up detritus. I finally see the little boy he's been hiding, and he's brilliant.

HOME?

On the plane, I think about that evening at the beach with Dodger, and it makes me smile. I imagine him getting better at swimming with every weekly trip to the swimming pool. I bet his English will be better than my Vietnamese pretty soon, as all the volunteers at that orphanage are foreign. All those battered, broken, but bouncy kids in one place, ready to rebound back into the world to prove their resilience. I loved it, especially when the little rascals got out of hand and I saw Dodger putting them in their place, as the born leader he is. I would have stayed to help but unfortunately I'm not that good a person.

I was once a fresh-faced traveller; friendly, sociable and naive in all the best ways. I would go out of my way to do a favour for a friend, and I would allow a sincere and heartfelt conversation to develop on the first night I met someone. I would spill my soul, and listen with empathy as they spilled theirs. Friends for a week or friends for a year, they were all ephemeral. I farewelled those who I felt a deep, spiritual connection with again and again, over and over. I guess the goodbyes just started to hurt, so I stopped saying hello. I don't dislike my misery. I wallow in it. It's the only friend I have left.

I complain about the cold as soon as I get off the plane. I accidentally line up in the queue for foreigners, killing forty minutes of my life that I didn't want anyway. I look around at London for a while, thinking of more ways to waste minutes of my mortality while I wait for my bus. I buy a coffee for a million pounds and head outside to the smoking area. I'm instantly smacked in the face by health and safety procedures, protocol, politeness, giving way, apologising for nothing, thanking for nothing, babying me at every turn and ordering me around. Someone shouts at me for disobeying a one-way system and I tell them I don't speak English in Vietnamese. I smoke a cigarette in the silence of a lack of chaos and stimulation. My head starts ringing, and I go to a phonebox to answer it. I dial the mobile number my mum has had for the last fifteen years.

"Hello?" The soothing, familiar voice that used to tuck me in at night.

"Hey mum, it's me."

"Hello darling! How are you?" She doesn't rub it in my face that I've been AWOL for months and she's probably been worried sick.

"I'm sorry I haven't called in so long. Things were a bit mad."

"Oh sweetheart it's so good to hear from you! How are you?"

"I'm good, mum. I was working some things out but I feel better now."

"Where are you?"

"I've been thinking about coming home to visit you for a bit."

"Oh lovely! Please do! When are you thinking of coming?" I look around at the crowds and ask myself the same question.

"In a couple of months, maybe? I promise I'll let you know as soon as possible. I've just got a few more things to do."

"Is everything okay in Vietnam?"

"I'm not gonna lie, mum. I've been doing nothing great. I've been doing nothing great for a while now. It's not been ideal if I'm honest, so I'm working on changing it." The true words are the right words.

"What is it? What have you been up to?"

"It's okay mum. I'm doing something worthwhile now."

"Oh, lovely. I'm so glad sweetheart. And what-"

"Mum I'm sorry, I'll call you properly in a couple of days okay? And we can have a proper chat, yeah?"

"Ok great, darling, please do."

"I've gotta go now. I love you mum."

"I love you too sweetheart. Call me."

"I promise!"

"Bye love."

"Bye mum."

I put the phone down, feeling like I'd made a social contract. 'I'm doing something worthwhile now' was more than a way to make the woman who birthed and nurtured me feel more at ease with her son's lack of character. I've said it now, so I guess I have to make it true for her. I walk back into the airport and look at the departures board. Kuala Lumpur, San Francisco, Rome, Bogota, Beijing, Brasilia, Amsterdam, Manila, Ho Chi Minh City. Two and a half hours until the flight leaves. Airline desk, tickets bought, check-in, bag-drop, security check, gate 47. Let's try this again.